Molly and her
mum go to show
the dentist
Molly's teeth.

"What lovely teeth!" says
Dr Brushwell.
"Can I have a closer look?"

"Shall we both look at your teeth with this tiny mirror?" Dr Brushwell asks.

Dr Brushwell gives Molly a toothbrush to keep her teeth shiny and clean.

"Bye-bye, Molly, brush well!" he says.

Molly can't wait to
use her new toothbrush.
"I like going to the dentist,"
says Molly, "but best of all . . .

. . . I like brushing my teeth!"